For Mekdes and Zinash
—NG

For my mother,
Carmen Lydia Velasquez
—EV

Special thanks to composer Keith Ward
for the original music score on the CD.

ZONDERKIDZ

Voices of Christmas
Copyright © 2009 by Nikki Grimes
Illustrations © 2009 by Eric Velasquez

Requests for information should be addressed to:
Zonderkidz, Grand Rapids, Michigan 49530

Library of Congress Cataloging-in-Publication Data

Grimes, Nikki.
     Voices of Christmas / by Nikki Grimes.
        p. cm.
     Includes bibliographical references.
     ISBN 978-0-310-71192-6 (jacketed hardcover)
     1. Jesus Christ--Nativity--Juvenile literature. I. Title.

    BT315.3.G75 2006
    232.92--dc22   2006012787

Editor: Betsy Flikkema
Art direction and design: Kris Nelson

Printed in China

09 10 11 12 • 5 4 3 2 1

Voices
OF
Christmas

Written by
Nikki Grimes

Illustrated by
Eric Velasquez

ZONDERVAN.com/
AUTHORTRACKER
follow your favorite authors

Gabriel

Hush! The hour is late.

Nazareth lies sleeping,
and I wait for my Lord's signal
to once again go
to earth below.
When last I went, my words
were for Zechariah.
Now, I pace the halls of heaven
memorizing a message
for Mary.
(Every archangel I see
envies me!)
I must get the message right:
The Light of the World
is on his way!
What will Mary say
when I tell her?

I wonder what he'll look like,
God wrapped in baby's skin,
stepping from Eternity into Time?
How will he hide his glory?
How will he hold it all in?

Ah! There! The bells chime
and I must go.
And so
I spread my wings, and spring
from heaven's balcony.

God to a town in Galilee called Nazareth, to a virgin.

Mary

...er and said, "Greetings, favored one! The Lord is with you."

He is gone now,
but still my bedroom walls beam
brighter than moonrise.
My spine tingles from his touch.
Such heat pulsing from white light!
Voice deeper than echo,
he spoke to me
familiar words from prophecy:
"The Master is sending Man
a baby. A boy. A King. His Son!"
Then he added impossibly,
"You, Mary, will be the one
he calls Mother."
Then he was gone!
Now I, alone, remain
rooted to this dirt floor,
dizzy with wonder,
pinching my wrist,
waiting to wake
from this dream.

Joseph

Her husband Joseph, being a righteous man an

nwilling to expose her to public disgrace, planned to **dismiss her** quietly.

There is little sleep
for me tonight,
only tossing and turning
and mourning over Mary.
I'll have to send her away now.
How could I marry a girl
who is having someone else's baby?
Why has she done this to me?
If only I could sleep, maybe then
I could find answers in my dreams.
"Joseph," an angel says to me,
"take Mary as your wife.
The life inside of her
comes from The Everlasting One.
He is the Messiah, God's own Son
and you will call him Jesus."
Moments later I awake,
certain as sky that I've had
more than a dream.
I wait for this mighty mystery
to unfold.
For now, this one thing I know:
I am ready now to do
whatever Jehovah
tells me to.

Elizabeth

In those days **Mary** went with haste to a **Judea**

...own in the hill country, where she entered the house of Zechariah and greeted Elizabeth.

Heavy as I am,
I sail above the ground.
My magic carpet? Joy!
Any day now, I will have a boy,
God be praised!
What will Cousin Mary say,
me an old woman
with a baby on the way—
a boy who will lead men
to the Messiah?
I haven't long to ponder.
Mary arrives at my door
with news more miraculous than mine.
The babe in my belly leaps
to let me know
it is Mary's boy
mine will lead men to,
Mary's son who will be
the Holy One.
Then, all at once,
my voice rings out with prophecy:
"Hear me, Mary:
More than any other woman,
you are blessed."

Zechariah

"Do not be afraid, Zechariah, for your prayer
Your wife Elizabeth will bear you a son, and y

Yes, I am a dim-witted man,
dismissing an answer to prayer!
I did not believe Gabriel,
whom God sent to tell me
I'd be a father
in my old age.
And, since I would not
accept his words,
he stole mine
and left me silent
for nine, long months.
But once my boy was born,
words of rejoicing ripped
my veil of silence in two:
"Blessed be you, Lord God of Israel!"
I lifted my son toward heaven,
happy at the sound of his cry.
"I name you John," I said.
"And you, child, will be called
the prophet of the Most High.
You will prepare his way!"
From that day to this,
I have praised the Lord
without ceasing,
never to be silent again.

...as been heard.
...ill name him **John.**"
...Zechariah said to the angel, "How will I know this is so?"

Neighbor

In those days a **decree** went out from Emperc

Joseph also went from the town of Nazareth

...Augustus that all the world should be registered ... alilee to Judea, to the city of David called **Bethlehem.**

I saw her,
belly ripe to the touch,
her baby ready to drop
at any time.
And yes, I watched Joseph
cinching wineskins
to his donkey's saddle,
wondered why
he was dragging that poor girl
to Bethlehem.
Someone from the family
had to go, of course.
The Emperor made it plain:
all must register for the Census.
But surely Joseph could have
registered for them both.
Still, gossips say
Mary would not stay behind.
God keep them both.
The journey ahead
is a maze of rough road
and danger in the dark.
I fear their future
is marked with trouble.

The Innkeeper

And she gave birth to her firstborn son an

See here!

My inn is splitting its sides
with travelers,
the spare rooms swallowed up
by Roman soldiers, merchants,
and who knows who!
Don't blame me.
The young girl with belly
round as a drum
was not the only one
forced to come to Bethlehem.
But, since her husband
rapped upon my door,
I led them to a dry spot
in my stable,
and a bed of hay
on which to lay themselves.
It was the most I could offer,
other than to share
my own, warm room.
And who would care
to do that for strangers?
It's not as if they were royalty, right?
A stable would do for the night.

rapped him in bands of cloth, and laid him in a manger, because there was **no place for them** in the inn.

Shepherd

In that region there were shepherds living in th

elds, **keeping watch** over their flock by night.

Who could forget it?

The sky a cloak of velvet
stitched with stars, we shepherds
studied the heavens
while our sweet sheep rested safe
in the pen we'd built of whatever rocks
we could find. And there I was
leaning against a tree
cradling Moriah, a wee lamb
tuckered out from wandering off again.
My feet burned from the chase.
Then suddenly the sky blazed
with the light of an angel.
"Be not afraid," he said.
"To you is born this day
a Savior, the Messiah."
Moriah stirred at this voice like thunder.

I wondered, Why come to us?
We are not priests. But then,
I remembered King David,
how God drew near to him who
once was a shepherd too.
"You will find the child lying
in a manger," the angel said.
We fled from the hills
to search for
this wonder, this holy child.
You ask if we found him.
What? Did you not hear us
shout for joy?

Gaspar

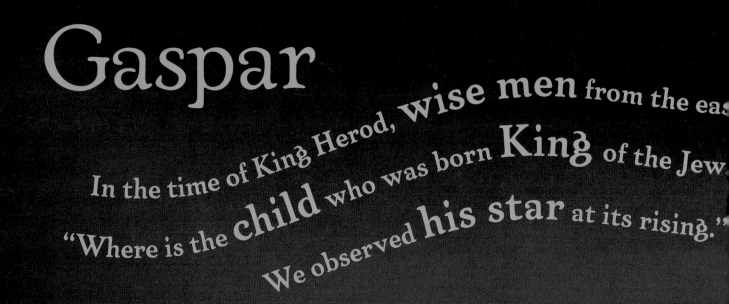

In the time of King Herod, wise men from the east
"Where is the child who was born King of the Jew
We observed his star at its rising."

All those years of poring over
charts and scrolls on astronomy,
then suddenly, it was as if
the Morning Star
leapt from the page
and rose into the sky.
I have waited for its appearing
so long, I know its shape by heart.
This star marks the Messiah's birth.
God, at last, has come to earth
and I must find him!
"Brothers, it is time for us
to begin the journey
for which we were born.
Pack quickly and take
a gift for the King.
We leave in the morning."

ame to Jerusalem, asking,

Herod

When King Herod heard this, he was frightened and learned fro

Then Herod secretly called for the wise men
them the exact time when the star had appeared.

Midnight finds me twisted
on my golden bed
my sickly, sagging body
a bundle of fever and fear
Still, I am king! Do you hear?
I shake my fist at Heaven
remembering the words
of those blasted magi
When were they here?
Days ago? Or maybe weeks
All I know for certain
is that they spoke of a star
rising in the sky, marking a holy birth—
King of the Jews, come to earth
To take my place? Never.
I, alone, am king
"Find him for me," I told them
And they agreed
"I need to worship him," I lied.
Why do they not return?
Never mind. I'll find a way
to rid the land
of this star-marked boy
His death will be my joy

Melchior

And **there,** ahead of them, went the **star** that the

until it stopped over the plac

had seen at its **rising,** where the **child** was.

I might be mistaken,
but my heart seems
to beat more wildly
with every step we take
toward Bethlehem.
The Holy Family journeyed here,
beneath the path of the star.
"Tut-tut!" We urge our camels over
miles of sand, sun-baked mud,
and rock, until the fertile foothills
of the Shephelah are within sight.
There, the star seems frozen
in the sky, and I sense
the end of our search is near.
My brothers fear
the wrath of Herod,
for I have told them
we cannot return to his palace
as promised.
An angel warned me in a dream
that Herod means
to harm the Child,
and we dare not be the arrows
shot from Herod's bow.
"Tut-tut!
Come on, my lovely.
The jewel of Bethlehem
sparkles up ahead."

Simeon

Now there was a man in Jerusalem whose name was Simeon this man was **righteous** and devout, looking forward to the **consolation** of Israel

No priestly robes hang from my frame.

I am the same as you,
an ordinary man—
well, wrinkled, of course,
and of failing sight.
But the Spirit yet whispers to me
in the night, or at dawn.
Why? Because I love his Word,
his voice, and serve him by choice.
Last I heard him speak,
I hurried to the temple to seek
a couple offering their son
for God's blessing.
Shrouded in light, I knew
this child was the One!
Here was the promise
Jehovah made to me,
that I would see the Messiah
before I died!
I quickly made my arms
a living cradle
for the babe to rest in.
"This child," I said, "is destined
for the falling and rising of many."
"Watch," I told Mary.
"With each tomorrow,
your heart will swell
with blessing and with sorrow."
As for me, having seen the Messiah's face,
I am ready, Lord, to come home to you.
Hallelu!

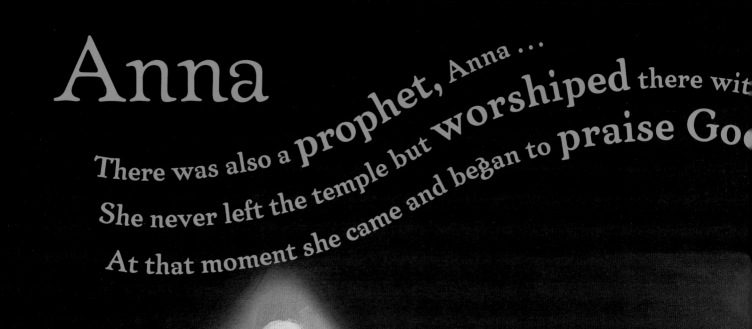

Anna

There was also a **prophet**, Anna...

She never left the temple but **worshiped** there wit...

At that moment she came and began to **praise** Go...

...asting and prayer night and day.
...nd to speak about the child.

I have welcomed the serene
routine of prayer, fasting, and worship
in the temple for sixty years.
But now, it appears, this day
will be like no other.
I come upon a father and mother
presenting their boy to the Lord.
I glimpse his sparkling eyes,
and my withered hand flies
to my chest.
I fight to catch my breath.
It is the Savior
bundled in Simeon's arms!
"Look! Here!" I cry out,
and my voice careens
through the temple courtyard.
"All you who seek
the redemption of Jerusalem,
look no further.
He is found!"
And all around,
young worshipers wonder
at the words
of this old woman.
But I know.
I know!

Balthasar

Then, opening their **treasure chest**, they offere

We enter the courtyard
where Mary bounces the baby
on her knee,
and my greedy eyes study
every inch of God's small son.
My ears tingle at the sound
of his giggle,
and all my mouth can manage
is "Master!"
I dig into my travel pouch
and pull out a gift of gold
which seemed generous,
till now.
But how could this trifle
begin to be enough
for the Savior of the world?

You

The woman said to him,
"I know that **Messiah** is coming."
... Jesus said to her, "I am he."

And who are you?

Not an angel, no.
Nor Herod.
But perhaps you are
a magi, mapping the miracle
on a chart of stars;
a shepherd
trading sleep
for a chance to seek
a golden child
in swaddling clothes;
a Simeon
who has hoped for a lifetime
to find the one called
Emmanuel, God with us.
Or are you like Mary,
prayerfully waiting
for the King of Kings
to be born in you?
Well, He is here!
Sing! Sing "O, Holy Night."
Run toward His Light!